This diary belongs to:

Pippa Morgan

HANDS OFF !!

Love and Chicken Nuggets

by Annie Kelsey

sourcebooks
jabberwocky

Published by Sourcebooks Jabberwocky, an imprint of Sourcebooks, Inc.
P.O. Box 4410, Naperville, Illinois 60567-4410
(630) 961-3900
Fax: (630) 961-2168
www.sourcebooks.com

Originally published in 2015 in Great Britain by Scholastic Ltd.

Library of Congress Cataloging-in-Publication data is on file with the publisher.

Source of Production: LSC Communications, Crawfordsville, IN, USA
Date of Production: November 2019
Run Number: POD

Printed and bound in the United States of America.
POD 10 9 8 7 6 5 4 3 2

With thanks and
chicken nuggets to
Kate Cary

Tuesday, Feb. 4

I wanted to start this brand-new diary with some really exciting news, like I've been invited to become a blindfolded trapeze artist for Zippy's Flying Circus or I've just won the world record for eating the most chicken nuggets while hopping on one leg or I've learned how to speak double Dutch. But no. Instead, I have to start this diary with the Most Depressing News in the History of Diaries.

Ever.

Our teacher, Mr. Bacon, wants us to do—wait for it—a Valentine's Day project.

Can you believe it???

Blargh!

(I've opened my *Exploring Japan* book and placed it on my desk in front of me so Mr. Bacon can't see me writing in my diary.)

What's so special about Valentine's Day? It's just a day when grown-ups get all gooey over each other. It's full of sappy movies on TV and icky love songs on the radio. *yawn* And there are the cards. The stores are full of them. They're ALL red and pink and covered in hearts. I tried to find the silliest one in the supermarket yesterday while Mom was buying vegetables.

The top three were:

1. A picture of a pizza with "Roses are red, violets are blue, this may be cheesy but I love you."

2. "We go together like peanut butter and jelly."

3. "I love you more than words can say." (I can't imagine *ever* feeling *anything* I couldn't say with words. Even if it's only made-up words, like when I feel ickerly-wickerly or fizzulated.)

Catie just leaned over to whisper that I'm always fizzulated.

STOP PEEKING AT MY DIARY, CATIE!

Okay! (Catie wrote that.)

(I've put Catie's *Exploring Japan* book on the desk between us so she can't see me either. She keeps giggling and pretending to peep over the top.)
  Since my best friend, Rachel, moved away to Scotland, Catie has become my second-favorite person in the

Catie

whole world (even if she *is* a PEEKER). We don't agree on *everything* though. For example: my favorite TV show is *CopShop* and her favorite TV show is *Celebrity Gymnast*. (I watched *CelebGym* with her last week. An ancient newscaster fell off the balance beam, and a TV chef got stuck on the parallel bars and had to be helped down. He was dangling over the top bar shouting, "Save me! I 'ave been skewered!" in a really French accent. It reminded me of the time me and Mom tried flipping pancakes and mine landed on the clothes-drying rack and hung there like a floppy omelette. I guess *CelebGym* is pretty funny, but it's not as good as *CopShop*.)

Mr. Bacon is writing a list on the whiteboard. He's written ♡♡ "Valentine's Day Project Ideas" ♡♡ at the top and drawn big hearts on either side with a pink marker! I hope he doesn't want us to write about *boys*. Boys are annoying. Some of them are okay, but mostly they just want to talk about soccer and sniff. Boys must have super-weird noses. I only sniff when I have a cold, but *boys* sniff ALL THE TIME.

Ha-ha! Jason Matlock is standing on his chair. Again. He did the same thing last week and Mr. Bacon had to get him down by promising him he could run around the playground five times. Mom says that some boys are like puppies—they need lots of food and lots of exercise. She says that school is the worst place for them because if they can't run around, they get restless and start chewing on the furniture. Maybe Jason's mom should send him to school with a squeaky toy.

While Mr. Bacon is talking Jason down, I can write my own list.

Why Boys Are Annoying

1. They push people on the playground.

2. They are sloppy eaters.

3. They talk in class. (I write in my diary during class, but that doesn't distract anyone.)

4. They like soccer.

5. They think burping is funny.

When do boys stop being a pain? I guess when they grow up. Mr. Bacon doesn't push the other teachers on the playground. But Dad still likes soccer, and he used to be a sloppy eater and burp until Mom told him not to. Was that why they got divorced? Did Dad want to be able to burp at dinnertime? He's got a girlfriend now. She's called Faye.

I wonder if she lets him burp when they go out for dinner?

When I know her better, I'll ask her.

Later (in the kitchen waiting for Mom to fry pizza for dinner)

I was TOTALLY wrong about Mr. Bacon's Valentine's Day project. It's not sappy at all! His whiteboard list was great. It looked like this:

Things you might LOVE to write about:

ANYTHING YOU LOVE!!!

And he underlined "ANYTHING" four times. Best. List. Ever.☺

So I can write about anything I love! Like fried pizza or going to the movies or Disneyland (where I've never been but I'm definitely going one day).

   This is going to be fab!

The only hard part will be deciding what NOT to write about. I love SOOOOOOOO MANY things!!!! But Mr. Bacon says we can only write about three. Only *three*!

Valentine's Day Project Ideas

Detectives: (like Detective Mike Hatchett from *CopShop*) If it wasn't for detectives, there would be criminals EVERYWHERE!

Dogs: Dogs are the best. If I had a dog, I'd call it Popcorn. I could train Popcorn to find my hair ties. I'm always losing them.

Astronauts: Imagine floating in space! By the time I'm grown up, I'll probably be able to go to Mars. SO awesome!

The Playground at the Park: I've had some of my best ideas while swinging on the swings. Flying up and down makes my brain think better thoughts. It also makes my stomach feel whooshy and tickly. I love it!

The Circus: I want to be a trapeze artist. I also want to be a lion tamer. (Except circuses don't have lions anymore. Maybe I could tame teachers instead.)

Tiffany J: She's the best pop star in the world. I was going to be just like her until I realized I can't sing. But I can dance really well, so I guess I could be one of her backup dancers.

Chicken Nuggets: BEST food in the world. The person who invented chicken nuggets is a GENIUS.

Ooh, got to go. I can smell fried pizza burning!

Wednesday, Feb. 5

I can't believe I ever thought Valentine's Day was sappy. Mr. Bacon's just been teaching us about Saint Valentine, who was *really* brave and not at all sappy.

He was an ancient Roman and he was like the Roman version of a priest and he used to marry people in secret so that the emperor couldn't send them to war. Married men weren't allowed to fight because they had families to look after. But the army was running out of soldiers, so the emperor made a law which said people weren't *allowed* to get married anymore.

So Saint Valentine secretly married lots of people (he didn't marry them himself, he just did the minister-y part with the "I do's"). But the emperor found out and got so mad that he cut Valentine's head off. Then Valentine became a saint.

He was SO brave. Imagine wanting to help people so much that you don't mind getting your head cut off. I don't think I could ever be that brave. Saint Valentine is totally my new hero.

I'm imagining being Saint Valentine (*before* he got his head cut off). I'm marrying a couple in secret. Soldiers are marching up and down in the streets, looking for men to join the army. I'm performing the ceremony in a cellar.

There are flaming torches on the wall and the cellar's all flickery with light. We have to whisper so no one can hear us. I've just done the part where I say, "You are now husband and wife," and a soldier bursts in and points at the man and says, "You have to join the army!" and I step forward and say, "He can't. He's *married!*"

That would be the coolest wedding ever.
☺☺☺

Mom and Dad's wedding didn't look anything
like that. I've seen the photos. They didn't get
married in a cellar in Rome. They got married
on a beach in Portugal. Which is pretty cool.
We went back to the beach when I was four.
I don't really remember it, except Mom and
Dad stood in the sea and kissed—ew!!

Wow! Mom and Dad used to love each other!
I'd forgotten that. It feels like they've been
divorced forever, even though it was only last
year. Now that Dad's seeing Faye, he's happier
than he's been for a long time. But Mom's

still alone. She's got me, but that's not the same as having a husband.

What would Saint Valentine do?

I know! He'd *find* her a husband! And if Saint Valentine can do it, so can I! That's going to be my *real* Valentine's project: I'm going to get Mom married by February 14 so she doesn't have to watch the sappy movies and listen to the stupid love songs by herself. It doesn't give me long—TEN DAYS!!! But if I try really hard, I know I can do it.

I'm going to make Saint Valentine SO proud! ☺

Later

Catie's at band practice, and I'm hiding from Mrs. Khan in the coatroom. Mrs. Khan's the lunch lady. She makes everyone go outside at recess, but it's freezing and I forgot to bring my mittens.

As soon as I got to school, I told Catie about my plan to find Mom a husband by Valentine's Day. She thinks it's SO romantic. She suggested looking for a husband on the Internet, but Mom tried online dating before Christmas and didn't like it. She said that it was like putting your hand in a box of snakes, hoping to find a diamond necklace. I need to find Mom someone *real* but

I don't think she knows any real-life men apart from Dad, and Dad's got Faye now.

Just before the attendance bell rang, Julie and Jennifer asked me and Catie if we'd decided what we were going to talk about for our *official* Valentine's project. Julie said they had persuaded Mr. Bacon to let them do a joint project because they are identical twins and love identical things. Jennifer said they were going to talk about karaoke, trampolining, and karate.

Then Catie told them what she was going to talk about.

What Catie Loves

1. The color pink. (I should have guessed. Catie's bedroom is so pink it glows.)

2. Playing the trombone. (Catie has trombone lessons but I've never heard her play.)

3. Monkeys. (I didn't expect THAT!)

ME: *Monkeys?*

CATIE: *(shrugging)* Why not?

ME: You never mentioned you loved monkeys before.

CATIE: You never asked.

ME: *(remembering to always ask people how they feel about monkeys in the future)* Any special type of monkey?

CATIE: Cute ones. There'll be squirrel monkeys at the zoo tomorrow. I can take photos for my project.

THE ZOO! Our school trip is *tomorrow!* I've been thinking so hard about Valentine's projects I'd almost forgotten! Squeeeeee! I'm SO excited!

My Favorite Animals

1. Tigers (because they're orange and striped—I wish I was orange and striped)

2. Komodo dragons (because they can bite off your fingers if they want)

3. Meerkats (because when they stand on their hind legs, they look like worried little businessmen waiting for a train)

4. Giant tortoises (I totally have to ride on the back of a giant tortoise one day)

5. Otters (Who doesn't love otters? They are *so* ottery.)

Later, when the twins had gone to get the class roster, Catie asked me what I was going to talk about for my project.

ME: (*thinking hard*) The swings in the park. (*thinking harder*) Detectives.

CATIE: Like Sherlock Holmes?

ME: No. Like the ones on *CopShop*. They are cool. Especially Detective Hatchett. I am SO going to be a police detective when I grow up.

CATIE: What's the third thing you love?

ME: Chicken nuggets. I *really* love them.

CATIE: Oh. I've never had a chicken nugget before.

ME: *(blinking fiercely to stop my eyes from popping out of my head)* What?! Not a single one?!?!

CATIE: *(shaking her head)* No. Never.

Now I have TWO extra Valentine's projects:

1. Find Mom a husband by February 14.

2. Get Catie to taste chicken nuggets for the first time ever.

Laterer (squinting because it's after bedtime and my night-light isn't very bright)

I'm trying to get to sleep, but I'm too excited about the zoo trip.

Catie's going to get some great monkey photos for her Valentine's Day project. I definitely need to start collecting stuff for my project soon. I wish I could show the class an episode of *CopShop*.

I watched it tonight and Detective Hatchett had to go undercover at a fish-and-chips shop to stop a gang of fish smugglers. The best part was when he barged into the gang leader's office and threw off his apron and showed his ID. "I'm Hatchett, *Detective* Hatchett."

The gang leader looked so shocked. He tried to climb out of the window but Detective Hatchett chased him down and handcuffed him.

Mr. Bacon probably wouldn't let me show a whole episode. ☹ Maybe I could find a picture of Detective Hatchett on the Internet and print it out.

Why I Love Detectives

1. They always get the bad guys.

2. They are smart. Whenever Detective

Hatchett interrogates a suspect, he always gets the information he wants. (Mom would make a great detective. I can't hide anything from her. When I was little I thought she was a mind reader.)

3. They get to go undercover, which means they can be anything they want. (Like the time Detective Hatchett pretended to be a dolphin trainer at a Caribbean resort. He actually got to ride on the back of a dolphin. How cool is that?)

4. They use sirens on their cars. (Me and Mom could get to downtown in five minutes if we had a siren.)

I can hear Mom coming upstairs. I'd better hide my diary. She always comes in to kiss me good night.

Thursday, Feb. 6

SCHOOL TRIP DAY!!!!

Guess what? Catie's mom is one of the parents helping out on the trip! She decided to volunteer at the last minute. I wish my mom could have come too, but she's working today.

We're on the bus RIGHT NOW. I am SO excited. I'm squished up against the window beside Darren. He's busy playing a game on his phone, which means I can write in my diary in peace. ☺

Catie's sitting in front of me, next to her mom, trying to teach her everyone's name. (I

don't think Mrs. Brown is a very quick learner —
she keeps getting Julie and Jennifer mixed up
and she thinks Jason is called James.)

Jason is totally hyper. As soon as Mrs.
Brown began to shoo us on to the bus, he
started doing monkey impressions.

Jennifer and Julie thought it was funny
and kept giggling as they followed him down
the aisle, but me and Catie ignored him. We
were whispering, trying to think up a plan to
get Mom a husband by Valentine's Day.

ME: I could put flyers in my neighbors'
mailboxes.

CATIE: I'm not sure your mom would like that.

(*Jason starts climbing over the seat, whooping like a baboon.*)

ME: I could auction her on eBay.

CATIE: I don't think you're allowed to sell your mom.

ME: It wouldn't *really* be selling. More like advertising.

(*Jason starts swinging from a luggage rack while Mrs. B begs him to get down.*)

MRS. B: (*looking panicked*) Is James dangerous?

JULIE: Who, *Jason?* No. He's just energetic.

JASON: My mom says if you ~~plugged me into an electric outlet,~~ you could ~~power a billion toasters.~~

MRS. B: *(looking more panicked)* Let's stay away from electric outlets, okay?

Today is going to be fantastic! Jennifer and Julie have a gazillion jelly beans. Me and Catie both have our phones. Catie's going to take pictures of monkeys for her project and I'm going to take pictures of EVERYTHING. She's been telling me some interesting monkey facts:

- They can take the lids off jars (she saw it in a documentary).

- They can catch ants on sticks (same documentary).

- They can swing by their tails (not even Jason can do that).

I wish I had a tail. That would be so much fun. I could use it to write my homework while I was texting with my thumbs.

The catching-ants-with-sticks thing isn't totally great because when they've caught them, they eat them. ALIVE! Can you imagine having ants running over your tongue? Ew! If I was a monkey, I'd stick to bananas.

Oh wow! I just saw the sign for the zoo. I can  see the entrance ahead. We're heading into the parking lot! Today is going to be the best day ever!

Later

We are having a break.

Julie and Jennifer have gone to wait in line for hot dogs and chips, and I'm sitting at a picnic table with Catie.

Poor Catie. She's still as white as a polar bear. But at least she's stopped trembling. I told Mr. Bacon that she didn't want to go to the reptile house. Snakes are NOT her favorite thing. But Mrs. Brown said she'd be okay. And Mr. Bacon said she'd better stick with the group. So she followed me in, like we were heading into a dungeon full of trolls.

She says snakes give her the "heebie-jeebies." Isn't that the BEST word ever? I hope something gives me the heebie-jeebies one day; it sounds fun, although Catie says it isn't.

Why Snakes Give Catie the Heebie-Jeebies

1. They are wiggly.

2. They are hissy.

I said, "Is that all?" and she said, "Isn't that *enough*?" Then I pointed out that cats can be wiggly and hissy and Catie said, "But cats have legs," and I said, "Would you like snakes if *they* had legs?" but she just looked pale and didn't answer.

Personally, I love snakes. I wish I could slide along the ground on my belly and slither up drainpipes and under furniture. I told Catie, but she just stuck her fingers in her ears and la-la-la'ed at me. So I didn't tell her that I'd been wondering what it feels like to digest a live mouse really slowly. (Not that I'd want to, but it can't be worse than tongue-ants.)

ANYWAY.

In the reptile house, we stayed near Mrs. Brown. Jason kept being noisy, racing from one window to another staring at the snakes behind them. Catie mostly looked at her feet, especially when we neared the cobra (which was fantastic because it was rearing up with a big puffed-out neck like it was about to attack us).

When we got to the boa constrictor, Mrs. Brown persuaded Catie to look at it because the boa was coiled up asleep. While Catie was peering nervously through the glass, I heard footsteps behind us. Then there was a sudden hiss and Catie screamed and leaped into the air like a mouse had run up her leg.

I turned just in time to see Jason racing out of the reptile house, laughing.

Catie was flapping her hands at the back of her neck screaming, "Get it off me! Get it off me!" While Mrs. Brown hurried after Jason, I tried to calm Catie down.

ME: There's nothing there. It was just Jason playing a trick.

CATIE: (shuddering) Something touched my neck!

ME: It was only Jason (which is *worse* than a snake, as far as I'm concerned).

CATIE: (eyes *brimming*) Are you sure?

ME: (*hugging Catie*) I promise.

Mr. Bacon was looking from across the hall, but I smiled at him to let him know it was okay and led Catie out of the reptile house.

Jason Matlock is horrible! I hope a tiger eats him.

The twins have promised not to let him near Catie for the rest of the trip. I'm going to make a Leaning Tower of Chips to cheer her up.

Laterer

I'm home now. Mom's vacuuming and I'm supposed to be washing up, but my diary comes first. Because there's SO MUCH to tell!

We ate lunch beside the giraffe exhibit. I kept expecting the giraffes to lean over the fence and steal my sandwiches. But they didn't. They just stalked around like Mom when she's wearing high heels.

I finally found out how they drink. They do the splits with their front legs and bend their heads down to the water. It looks really uncomfortable. I asked a zookeeper why they don't just give the giraffes tall water troughs, but she said that they like to "keep the habitat as natural as possible." I wonder if that's why you don't get silverware at McDonald's. I guess humans ate with their hands before restaurants were invented. Maybe McDonald's is just trying to keep it real.

ANYWAY.

Something amazing happened after lunch. I got to meet a real-life detective! At the ZOO! I totally didn't expect that.

First, the whole class was crowding around the elephant exhibit while Mr. Bacon told us how Asian elephants are more closely related to woolly mammoths than to African elephants.

Then we went to see the monkeys. Catie was so excited. She'd forgotten all about Jason and the reptile house (I think my Leaning Tower of Chips helped) and was beaming the biggest smile ever when I took photos of her in front of the squirrel monkeys. They were racing around behind the wire fence and it was hard to get a good picture, but then Catie turned around and called to them and they all stopped and looked at her. They stared at her with big, adoring eyes, like she was their Monkey Queen. I took the BEST photo!

Then Mr. Bacon split us up into teams to play Zoo Bingo. He gave each team a sheet with lots of pictures of different animals. He told us to find all the animals on the sheet and cross them off, then come back to the monkey house. Catie and I were on a team with the twins. He said we were responsible enough to go off by ourselves as long as we stuck together. Jason's group had to stay with Mrs. Brown.

The first picture was a penguin, and I remembered seeing a penguin sign near the gift shop. So I raced there, with Catie and the twins running behind me. Once we'd crossed off the penguins, Catie said she knew where the ostriches *and* the parakeets were. Then there was a frog on the sheet. And a snake.

The twins said we'd have to go back to the reptile house. Catie started looking pale again, but the twins offered to go inside while me and Catie waited outside. Then Catie said something AMAZING.

CATIE: I'm going in.

ME: (confused) But you're scared of snakes.

CATIE: I'm going in anyway. Mr. Bacon said we have to stick together.

And she just marched inside.
   I was so proud! She walked right past the snakes and headed toward the frogs. Me and

the twins had to run to keep up. Catie peered through the glass and pointed at a tiny orange frog hidden in the big green leaves. Then she turned around and pointed at the boa constrictor and said, "We can cross the *snake* off the sheet too."

She wasn't even trembling!

I was so proud that I took a picture of her in front of the boa constrictor as proof that Catie Brown is the Bravest Girl Ever.

We found all the other animals really quickly and raced back to the monkey house. Mr. Bacon was waiting on a bench, looking sleepy.

He stood up when he saw us running toward him.

ME: Are we first?

JULIE: We saw all the animals!

Catie handed him our sheet with all the pictures crossed out and I showed him my photo of Catie Being Brave in the reptile house.

Mr. Bacon smiled and said good job just as the other teams started appearing. While everyone was comparing sheets and checking to see who'd gotten all the animals, Mrs. Brown hurried down the path with Darren and Tom looking flustered.

MRS. BROWN: Is James here?

CATIE: You mean *JASON!*

MRS. BROWN: *(looking even more flustered)* Is *Jason* here?

MR. BACON: I haven't seen him.

MRS. BROWN: He slipped away while I was getting a rock out of my shoe.

Mr. Bacon started organizing new teams to go and search for Jason. Mrs. Brown kept apologizing, but Mr. Bacon told her that Jason got lost on every school trip. He did look worried though.

Everyone was talking at once, so Mr. Bacon could hardly make himself heard.

I was imagining Jason being carried around the elephant exhibit, wrapped in the trunk of an angry elephant. Then I wondered if he'd climbed in with the boa constrictor and was being quietly crushed to death. Then I looked into the monkey cage. I half expected to see him swinging through the branches. While I was picturing him swimming with the penguins, a tall man in an overcoat called to Mr. Bacon over my classmates' heads.

TALL MAN: Is anything wrong?

MR. BACON: We've lost one of our students.

TALL MAN: Can I help? I'm a police detective.

A DETECTIVE! My brain totally caught fire. I could hardly stand still. A real live detective! At the zoo!

Mr. Bacon looked relieved, and the detective started asking Mrs. Brown and Darren and Tom where they'd seen Jason last. (It was like a real interrogation! Except there were monkeys whooping in the background.) Then he headed back up the path with everyone following like he was the Pied Piper.

Jason was in the gift shop, *of course.* He was looking at the postcards and checking off the animals on his bingo sheet.

While the rest of the class crowded outside, Mr. Bacon and the detective went inside and fetched him.

Mrs. Brown looked so happy I thought she was going to hug Jason. Mr. Bacon kept shaking the detective's hand while shooting angry looks at Jason. Jason just shrugged and sniffed like he didn't know what the big deal was.

Then I had the best idea in the world!

I put my hand in the air and waved at the detective. "Can I interview you for my school project? *Pleeeassseeee!*"

The detective looked at Mr. Bacon.

Mr. Bacon said it was okay. He was already herding everyone (even Jason) back into the gift shop. So, while the group was buying postcards and pencil sharpeners shaped like tigers, I sat on a bench and interviewed a real live *detective*!

I was so nervous I could hardly speak, but then I imagined I was Mike Hatchett of the Fraud Squad. I got out my clipboard and checked my watch and said, "Interview beginning at thirteen fifty hours."

ME: What's your name, rank, and badge number? (All police officers have badge numbers. I learned that from *CopShop*.)

POLICEMAN: Burrows, Detective, number 22244.

ME: Where are you stationed?

DET. BURROWS: Barnsbury.

ME: Do you have a special detective badge? (Mike Hatchett would always check to make sure his witness is not an imposter.)

DET. BURROWS: (*showing me his badge*) Yes.

ME: Can you arrest people even when you're off duty?

DET. BURROWS: Yes.

ME: (I imagined Jason behind bars, then realized my mind was wandering. A *good* detective stays focused on her case, and my case was to find out everything I could about Detective Burrows.) What are you doing at the zoo? Are you working undercover?

DET. BURROWS: (*nodding to a woman and a young boy who are watching the monkeys*) No, it's my day off, so I took my family out.

ME: (*suspicious*) How do I know they're not part of your undercover team?

DET. BURROWS: (*waving at the young boy, who waves back*) We don't recruit five-year-olds.

ME: (*refusing to be tricked that easily—the young boy might be a decoy*) What time did you leave the house?

DET. BURROWS: (*smiling*) Oh nine hundred hours precisely.

ME: Were you tailed?

DET. BURROWS: Only by the number twenty-six bus, but I managed to shake it off at the traffic lights.

ME: Do they train you to shake off tails at police school?

DET. BURROWS: It's the first thing we learn.

ME: What else do you learn? (Thorough questioning is important.)

DET. BURROWS: How to deal with members of the public, like you and your disappearing friend.

ME: He's not *my* friend.

I suddenly noticed Mr. Bacon waving at me from outside the gift shop as the rest of the class headed for the bus.

DET. BURROWS: I think your teacher wants you.

ME: He can wait. (Suddenly I knew how Detective Hatchett feels when his superintendent is giving him grief.)

Detective Burrows looked unconvinced, but I had too many questions to ask. This could be the most important case in my career!

ME: How many criminals have you caught?

DET. BURROWS: (*shaking his head*) I've lost count.

ME: Can you tell just by looking if someone's a criminal?

DET. BURROWS: Not by the way they look, but by the way they act. I can spot someone looking suspicious a mile away.

ME: (*pointing at Mr. Bacon, who's beckoning me fiercely*) Does Mr. Bacon look suspicious?

DET. BURROWS: No. He looks like he's in a

hurry. You'd better get going before you miss your bus.

ME: One last question.

DET. BURROWS: I need to join my family.

ME: What's the best thing about being a detective?

DET. BURROWS: Helping people.

I grinned. That was the best answer ever. It'll sound great in my presentation. I checked my watch again and said, "Interview terminated at fourteen hundred hours."

Detective Burrows got to his feet and smiled at me. "You'll make a good officer one day."

I beamed. "Thanks!" I can't wait to write *that* in my project.

I love detectives because one day I'm going to *be* one. (Or an acrobat or a lawyer or a rocket ship designer—I haven't *completely* decided.)

I sat next to Catie on the way home because Mrs. Brown wanted to sit by herself near the front. (She said she was tired and wanted to practice her "relaxation techniques.")

ME: Did you have fun, Catie?

CATIE: *(looking through the photos of her and the monkeys and the snake on my phone)* Best day EVER.

It *was* the best day ever. I interviewed a *real* detective! My Valentine's Day project is going to be fantastic! ☺ ☺ ☺

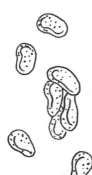

Now I need to start working on my other V-Day projects: chicken nuggets for Catie and a husband for Mom!

Friday, Feb. 7

I went jogging with Mom this morning. It was still <u>DARK</u>. The streetlights turned us orange, so I pretended that I was a tiger and we were running through a jungle. Mom told me to stop growling at other joggers. I told her that's what tigers do, but she said people didn't *want* to meet tigers on their morning jog. Who wouldn't want to meet a tiger? People are weird.

Mom took up jogging after Dad moved out. She said she was going to become a vegetarian too. Fortunately, she hasn't gotten around to that yet. I think I would die without bacon sandwiches. She *did* get around to having her hair cut, and she's started to listen to loud rock music. (REALLY loud rock music, especially when she's cooking dinner—you can feel the house throbbing. The other day, I went in to ask if dinner was ready and she was playing air guitar on a wooden spoon while the pasta was cooking. I joined in, playing drums on the kitchen table with chopsticks.)

ANYWAY.

While we were jogging through the park (without growling), I told Mom about Saint Valentine and how he had his head chopped off for marrying people.

MOM: (*jogging*) Serves him right.

ME: *(puffing)* Don't you want to get married again?

MOM: No.

ME: *(panicking about my Valentine's project)* Never?

MOM: Not right now.

ME: *(hopefully)* But one day?

MOM: Maybe.

I jogged quietly after that without growling or talking. How could Mom not want to get married? Did she *like* being alone? I worried all the way around the park. Then, as we headed down our street, I *realized*: she just hasn't found the right man yet! Don't worry, Saint Valentine! She'll change her mind once I've found her the Perfect Partner.

I'd better get ready for school. But first, I'm taking a selfie to show Catie. My face is still glowing from my run. I'm pinker than Catie's bedspread!

Later

I showed Catie my selfie as soon as I got to school. She laughed so much that Jason wanted to know what was so funny. But there's no way I'm showing *anyone* else a picture of me looking like ~~pink bubble gum.~~

Then Mr. Bacon came in, and after he'd taken attendance, he asked the class how our Valentine's Day projects were going. Freya put up her hand and said she loved so many things she couldn't decide which to choose. Tom said that he only loves soccer (*rolls eyes*) and he couldn't think of anything else. Jason asked if he could do a talk about the school vacation days because he loves them. Mr. Bacon told him he could. I bet Mr. Bacon loves school vacation days too because they give him a break from Jason. Then Jason asked Mr. Bacon what *he* loved. Mr. Bacon said, "I love soccer (*double eye-roll*) and history (*yawn*) and the countryside." Being old must be <u>really</u> boring.

Then Mandy Harrison put up her hand and asked why Mr. Bacon didn't love his *wife*. And Mr. Bacon said he didn't *have a* wife, and Mandy asked, "Why not?" And Mr. Bacon said, "I suppose I haven't met the right woman yet."

☺ ☺ ☺ ☺

My heart nearly burst with excitement!

OF COURSE!!!!!

My mom + Mr. Bacon = TRUE LOVE!!!!!

He is PERFECT for her! He's clever and kind and he's about the same height and he drives a car that is exactly the same shade of blue as Mom's car. They *must* be soul mates.

I have to get them together!

I put up my hand right away and asked when the next parent-teacher conference was. It would be the perfect way to get them to meet. But Mr. Bacon said it wasn't until next quarter.

NEXT *QUARTER*!

I've only got till next week!

Then Jason started flicking paper balls across his desk, and when Mr. Bacon told him to stop, Jason said, "Why?" and Mr. Bacon said, "BECAUSE IF YOU DON'T, I'M GOING TO SPEAK TO YOUR MOTHER."

That's when I had my SECOND brilliant idea. I told Catie about it on the playground at lunchtime.

ME: All I have to do is mess around in class and Mr. Bacon will *want* to speak to my mom.

CATIE: (*looking worried*) I don't think that's a good idea.

ME: It's a *great* idea! As soon as Mr. Bacon and Mom see each other, they'll fall in love.

CATIE: *(still looking worried)* But what if they don't?

ME: They *will!* Mr. Bacon's really nice and my mom is fab — she looks really cool now she's had her hair cut. I just know they'll like each other.

CATIE: What if he calls your *dad* instead?

ME: He won't!

Catie worries WAY too much. Once I've finished getting Mom a husband and shown Catie how wonderful chicken nuggets are, I'm going to start working on Catie's PMA. PMA = Positive Mental Attitude. Mrs. Allen, our PE teacher, goes on about it all the time. She thinks that if we believe we can run faster, we *will* run faster. I'm not sure that's totally true. After all, if *believing* things made them true, I'd have a pet tiger and I'd be able to fly. I'd also be able to sing like Tiffany J. But I think that *imagining* makes people happy; I know it makes *me* happy.

Last night, while I was doing my math homework, I imagined I went to see a Tiffany J concert and she asked me onstage to dance with her and I danced so well that she invited me backstage and we became really good friends and she insisted I stay with her on her private island. And the private island was fantastic. It had white, sandy beaches and palm trees and the bluest water ever, and Tiffany's villa was huge and had a swimming pool with its own waterslide.

And just as I was about to slide down

it, Mom asked me why math homework was making me smile so much. So I told her I was smiling because it was so easy. And guess what? It *was*.

ANYWAY.

I have to figure out how I can make Mr. Bacon SO angry at me on Monday that he wants to speak to Mom. Whenever he speaks to Jason's mom, he waits on the playground for her at the end of the day, then he takes her into school for "a word." (I bet it's more than *one* word.) So I have to persuade Mom to look pretty when she comes to pick me up on Monday.

I've never messed around in class before, but I know Mr. Bacon will forgive me as soon as he

sees Mom. I can just picture her standing at
the school gates—she'll
be wearing her pretty
floaty dress, and her
hair will be perfect, and
Mr. Bacon will see her
and stare like he's been hit by a love
arrow (like the ones you see on Valentine's
cards. I'm not sure what arrows have got to
do with love. Maybe in the old days, people
used to deliver their cards by firing them
through the mailbox).

I can't wait! Monday is going to be JUST like
one of those romantic movies Mom watches
where there's a big mix-up, and then the two
stars fall in love and live happily ever after.

Laterer

I'm at Dad's. And GUESS WHAT?
  MY ROOM IS LOOKING SUPER COOL!! ☺

When I got to the apartment, I could tell Dad
had a surprise. He opened the door looking all
smiley and secretive, like he does when he's
just bought my Christmas present and has
hidden it so I can't find out what it is. He
led me to my room and told me that he and
Faye had tried to brighten it up a little.
  I was SO happy when he opened the door.
  They had REALLY brightened it up! ☺ ☺
Last week, it was just a desk and a bed, with
two posters of Tiffany J on the walls. But
now there's a new yellow bedspread, a fluffy

rug just like Catie's, and cute
cushions everywhere. AND
there are fairy lights around the top of my bed
AND over my desk AND new orange curtains
AND a beanbag chair. Catie TOTALLY
has to visit now. I was kind of
embarrassed before because
Dad's apartment used
to look empty and sad,
but since he's been
going out with Faye, cushions and
rugs and pictures have started appearing
everywhere. There are even scented candles
beside the TV.

I gave Dad the biggest hug and told him I
loved it. Then he told me he was making Pizza

Faces for dinner. (Pizza Faces
are Dad's speciality. I get to
choose my own toppings and
put them on in the shape of
a face.)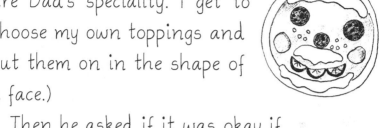

Then he asked if it was okay if
Faye came over after dinner.

I wasn't sure that I wanted to share Dad.
I'm only seeing him one night this week. But
then I looked at my new room. It was so pretty.
It would be mean not to share Dad after Faye
had been so kind. So I told him Faye should
have dinner with us, so that she could make
her own pizza face.

Dad grinned, and I felt happy because he
was happy.

Faye's here now in the kitchen, helping to make the pizza dough. It sounds like she and Dad are having fun. Dad keeps laughing and Faye keeps telling him to shush, then bursting into giggles. I didn't *know* old people giggled.

Mom needs someone to giggle with too. I can't wait till Monday morning so I can start messing around in class. Mr. Bacon will think I've been replaced by an alien, just like the scary movie I watched with Mom last weekend. Except I won't have laser eyes. That's a shame. If I had laser eyes, Mr. Bacon would speak to my mom right away.

Sunday, Feb. 9

Mom took Catie and me into town this afternoon so she could get her hair blow-dried. (I persuaded her that she deserves a treat because she works so hard. I didn't tell her I want her to look FABULOUS when she picks me up from school on Monday.)

While Mom was in the salon, Catie and I looked for things to photograph for our Valentine's project.

Catie took pictures of every pink dress and lipstick and pair of shoes that we saw. I decided that she needed something *interesting* for her project. Pink things are almost always boring. I told her to take a photo of my tongue, and she giggled and did. Unfortunately, I'd been sucking on candy and my tongue was blue, which made Catie giggle even more. Then I saw a really cool blob of bubble gum stuck to a lamppost. It was practically LUMINOUS PINK and it was shaped like an octopus. I showed it to Catie, but she said it wasn't pretty enough, and before I could point out that <u>interesting</u> is way better than <u>pretty</u>, she raced away down the street shouting, "Quick, Pip! I've found something perfect!"

By the time I caught up, she was standing outside the flower shop, her eyes wide and shining with joy. "Look!" she sighed dreamily as I caught up. "Aren't they *romantic*!"

She was staring at a huge bouquet of pink flowers in the window. Beside them was a sign that read, "Remember to send flowers to your Valentine!"

ICK!

Why does ANYONE send flowers on Valentine's Day? If I had a boyfriend (double-ick) I wouldn't want him to send me something that would sit in a vase and die while I watched. I'd want something useful, like a tiger or a trapeze or an astronaut's helmet. Or just chocolates. At least I could eat them.

I'm not sure Saint Valentine would

want to be remembered by a bunch of flowers. He'd be all, "I got my head cut off for THIS?"

But Catie took a picture anyway, and I just stared back sadly at the lamppost where the cool bubble gum was sitting, unloved and ignored.

Then Mom came out of the hairdresser's across the street and called to us, "Do you want to go to McDonald's?"

"Yeah!" I punched the air and raced toward her. It wasn't till Mom was herding us through the front door of McDonald's that I noticed Catie was looking nervous. While Mom joined the line at the counter, Catie hung back beside the door and stared around the

restaurant as though she'd landed on Mars and was expecting to see bug-eyed aliens at every table.

ME: *(whispering)* Are you okay?

CATIE: *(whispering too)* I've never been to a McDonald's before.

I didn't *actually* fall on the floor, but the

ground seemed to sway under me, like someone had flipped the world over.

ME: *Never? Why?*

CATIE: *(whispering even quieter)* Because my mom doesn't approve.

ME: *(doing a pretty good impression of a bug-eyed alien)* Is she a vegetarian?

CATIE: No. She just prefers healthy food.

Mom was inspecting the giant menu beside the counter. "What do you two want?" she called to us. I called back that we hadn't decided yet. This was my chance to get Catie to taste chicken nuggets for the very first time!

ME: You eat loads of healthy food at home, right? (*I knew the answer to this. Last time I had dinner at Catie's house, we had organic fish stew with brown rice. I didn't even know they made brown rice but apparently it's super healthy...*)

CATIE: I guess so.

ME: And all next week and the week after that?

CATIE: I guess.

ME: Then you can eat something unhealthy every now and then.

CATIE: *(staring at the pictures of burgers and fries above the counter)* Do they serve salad?

ME: *Salad?* No one eats salad at McDonald's.

I suddenly felt like a little cartoon devil sitting on Catie's shoulder and poking her with a big fork. I half expected an angelic Pippa to appear and persuade Catie that salad would be the best choice.

    I pushed the thought FAR away. Catie

needed to taste chicken nuggets. And it was my <u>duty</u> as her friend to make sure she ate one before she died. It would be so cruel of me to deprive her of one of the best experiences in the world. I said a quick prayer to Saint Valentine inside my head.

Dear Saint Valentine, please help me find the strength to make Catie fall in love with chicken nuggets. Thank you. Amen.

Then, bubbling with excitement, I grabbed her arm and marched her to Mom's side and told Mom that we were both having chicken nuggets.

Mom must have seen Catie shake like a

frightened rabbit because she asked her if that's what she really wanted. Catie looked at me, and I could see her swallow nervously before she said, "Yes, please."

"With large fries," I added.

I got Catie to a table before she could change her mind. We scooted over the seats so that we were sitting beside the window. "You're going to love chicken nuggets," I promised.

Catie's nose was twitching. "It does smell nice here."

Mom arrived and put down a tray loaded with nuggets and fries in front of Catie.

I grinned as Mom gave me my own tray. "This is perfect for my project." I got out my phone to take a pic.

Catie's eyes lit up. "Wait!" Quickly, she

arranged her nuggets into a heart shape and piled her fries in the middle. Then, as I was focusing my camera, she squeezed a tiny heart shape on top with her ketchup packet.

"That's amazing!" I took a photo. "My project's going to rock!"

Then Catie picked up a nugget and took a bite.

I held my breath and leaned forward in my seat, heart pounding.

What if nuggets tasted weird after a lifetime of organic fish stew?

I didn't dare blink in case I missed anything.

First Catie frowned; then she chewed; then she grinned and said, "They're delicious!"

My heart bumped up and down like a happy bunny in my chest.

ME: Do you *really* like them?

CATIE: I LOVE them!

It was like winning a trophy! I'd persuaded Catie Brown to taste her first chicken nugget! And she loved it!

It must be a sign from Saint Valentine. When Mr. Bacon and Mom meet, they will DEFINITELY fall in love.

I can't wait till Monday to put *Mission Troublemaker* into action.

Monday, Feb. 10

Messing around in class is hard work! I don't know how Jason is able to do it ALL THE TIME. He must have enough energy to power a *gazillion* toasters.

The last bell rang five minutes ago. If my plan had worked, I'd be standing on the playground next to Mr. Bacon now while he waited for my mom. But I'm not. I'm waiting in the coatroom, scribbling in my diary while Catie goes to the bathroom.

sigh

It's not like I didn't *TRY* to be bad. I spent all morning daydreaming instead of working. Mr. B kept telling me to do my work, but I kept staring out the window.

I thought he'd ask to speak to me when the lunch bell rang, but he just frowned at me, then headed off to the staff room.

On the playground I talked to Catie about it.

ME: Can I pretend to pinch you or something?

CATIE: But you'll look mean and you're not.

ME: I could pass you notes and whisper jokes to make you laugh.

CATIE: But then Mr. Bacon might speak to *my* mom instead of yours. What if he falls in love with the wrong mom?

That would be a disaster! But I wasn't going to give up. I thought so hard my brain hurt, and then I had an idea.

After lunch, I got all my books out of my cubby, and while Mr. Bacon was telling us about cherry blossom festivals in Japan, I started building a tower on my desk. I used books for the walls and balanced two rulers on top so I could build a second story. It was pretty impressive. Mr. Bacon didn't say anything until I got to the third story, by which time I couldn't see him from behind my tower.

MR. BACON: What are you doing, Pippa?

ME: Building a Japanese pagoda, Mr. Bacon.

MR. BACON: Why?

ME: I'm adding scenery to help you with the lesson.

MR. BACON: I don't need any help, thank you. Please take your pagoda down.

ME: Can I finish the roof first?

MR. BACON: (looking impatient) Would you like to stay after class and finish it?

ME: I can't. (*holding up two crayons*) Mr. and Mrs. Pencil need somewhere to live *now*. (*making the crayons walk across my desk and duck into the pagoda, then putting on a silly voice and waggling one of the crayons*) "Mr. Pencil, would you like a cup of coffee?" (*waggling the other one*) "No, thank you, Mrs. Pencil. I'm going to do some drawing." (*flashing Mr. Bacon a big smile*) Get it? Mr. Pencil is going to do some drawing!

Mr. Bacon frowned at me. "Pippa. You are disrupting class."

I felt myself blushing, but this was for a good cause, so I forced myself to sit up straight and said, "I was just trying to help."

Mr. B frowned even harder. "Please put Mr. and Mrs. Pencil away, take down your pagoda, and see me after class."

I thought I'd done it! Excitement was bubbling in my stomach as I turned my pagoda back into an ordinary pile of books and put Mr. and Mrs. Pencil to bed in my pencil case. He was *definitely* going to speak to my mom.

After class, I stood beside his desk while the rest of the class filed out. The twins gave me a sympathetic look; Catie crossed her fingers at me, wishing me luck. Jason stuck out his tongue and looked pleased that it was someone else in trouble, not him.

When they'd gone, Mr. Bacon got up and sat on the front of his desk. Then, with big sympathetic eyes like a rabbit, he said, "It's not like you to misbehave in class. Is anything wrong, Pippa?"

My mind started to whirl. *Of course there's something wrong! My mom's going to be alone on Valentine's Day and it's not fair because she's wonderful.* The words scrolled inside my head in big flashing letters, but I couldn't say them out loud because it would ruin my plan. So I shrugged.

Mr. Bacon tried playing detective. "Is everything okay at home?"

"It's fine." There was no way I wanted him

to think Mom wasn't the best mom in the world. (Which she is.)

He stared at me, looking puzzled. "Then why have you been messing around all day?"

I shrugged again.

Mr. Bacon shook his head, looking really confused. "You'd better go home, Pippa," he said. "Tomorrow I want you back to normal. Any more bad behavior and I'll have to speak to your parents."

ME: *(eagerly)* Mom's probably waiting outside. You can speak to her now.

MR. BACON: *(shaking his head)* You deserve

another chance. Let's just say you've had a bad day and see how tomorrow goes.

I dragged my feet all the way to the hall, where Catie and the twins were waiting.

CATIE: (*bouncing up and down excitedly*) Well? What did he say? Is he going to speak to your mom?

ME: (*dropping my backpack on the floor*) He's giving me another chance. I have to do it all over again tomorrow.

CATIE: (*hugging me*) Don't worry, Pippa! Go and ask your mom if you can come to my house. We'll make a plan that will DEFINITELY get you into trouble tomorrow.

(Julie and Jennifer look at each other like we'd gone nuts.)

JULIE: *(to me)* Did you *want* to get into trouble?

JENNIFER: I'd hate it if Mr. Bacon was angry with me.

CATIE: *(explaining)* Pippa's mom and Mr. Bacon *have* to fall in love by Valentine's Day.

The twins looked confused, so Catie explained some more. "Pippa's mom will have to spend

Valentine's Day by herself unless Mr. Bacon asks her to marry him."

I joined in. "And he won't ask her to marry him if he hasn't *met* her. So she *has* to come into school. Which means *I* have to get into trouble."

Catie went gooey-eyed. "It would be soooooo romantic." She led me toward the door. "Quick, Pippa. Ask your mom if you can come to my house. We have to make a plan!"

She asked the twins if they wanted to come too, but they have karate on Mondays. So I went to ask Mom.

Mom looked *so* pretty standing at the school gates. She'd worn her floaty dress. (I'd begged her last night. She wanted to know why, but I just told her that it makes me happy when she looks pretty.)

Oh, why didn't Mr. Bacon want to speak with her today? *wails*

But I'm <u>NOT</u> going to feel sad. Mr. Bacon was just being kind, which means he's even more perfect for Mom. And tonight, Catie and me will think up a brilliant plan for tomorrow.

Later

I was SO right!

BEST PLAN EVER!

Me and Catie have designed a whole *Troublemaking Toolkit*. It's crammed with ideas that will make Mr. Bacon SO mad he'll *have* to speak to Mom!

When we got to Catie's house, Mrs. Brown asked me to stay for dinner, so I phoned Mom to check that it was okay and we raced upstairs.

As soon as we were in Catie's bedroom she pulled out a big notepad. The first troublemaking ideas we had were silly (but they made us giggle):

1. Sing the national anthem during attendance.

2. Play Catie's trombone.

3. Pretend I'm a trapeze artist and swing from the fluorescent lights.

But then we started coming up with actual ideas.

PIPPA'S TROUBLEMAKING TOOLKIT

Put up my hand and ask questions every two minutes.

Pretend I can't hear Mr. Bacon and keep saying, "What?"

Go to the trash can to sharpen my pencil every five minutes.

Speak French. (I only know *bonjour* and *au revoir,* but that might be enough.)

 Tap my feet on the floor whenever Mr. Bacon starts speaking.

Keep blowing my nose.

Hum whenever Mr. Bacon turns his back.

Aren't they the BEST? If I do everything on the list, it'll drive Mr. B NUTS!

(Sorry, Mr. B, but you'll thank me for it on your wedding day.)

WEDDING DAY! I can picture it already!

There won't be any Roman soldiers or Portuguese fishermen. But it'll be somewhere nice. And afterward we could have a big party at that country hotel Mom and I stopped at on the way home from Center Parks last year. I can imagine all of our family and Mom's friends sitting at tables, all dressed up, while Mr. Bacon stands up to give a speech. He taps on his champagne glass to get everyone's attention, then he says:

"We're here today because of Pippa. Thanks

to her brilliant plan (and Catie's), I met the most wonderful woman in the world." Then he'd look dreamily at Mom and she'd gaze back romantically and everyone's eyes would fill up with tears because it's so sweet. And afterward, all our friends and relatives would crowd around me and Catie (we'd be wearing the prettiest bridesmaid dresses ever) and tell me how wonderful I am for getting Mom and Mr. Bacon together. I've got shivers of happiness just thinking about it!

Catie and I were so excited about our toolkit we couldn't stop chattering through dinner. I hardly noticed the three salads or the *brown* bread (blegh) or the organic sausages MADE OUT OF NUTS!!! I refused to try the blue cheese dressing though (it smelled like feet) and asked for ketchup instead. Ketchup made the salads taste MUCH better and gave me really nice-tasting burps all evening.

When Mom picked me up, she asked why I was grinning so much. I told her we'd had fun and I was looking forward to school in the morning. Which is totally true.

Please, Saint Valentine, help our plan work tomorrow! If Mr. Bacon and Mom fall in love, I promise I'll become a minister and marry hundreds and hundreds of people. It will be easy because there aren't any head-chopping emperors left. At least I don't think there are. I'll have to phone Dad and ask him...

Tuesday, Feb. 11

Oh no! _Disaster!_ The plan has gone horribly, horribly WRONG!

It's lunch break, and I'm squished into a bathroom stall so I can write in my diary. Catie is at her trombone lesson so I can't talk to her. ☹ ☹ What am I going to do? My life is officially over.

I did everything on the list! I put my hand up three times _before_ attendance and asked Mr. Bacon:

1.   How many ducks can you fit on an airplane?

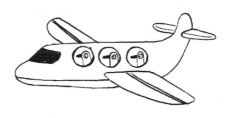

2. Can kangaroos hop on one leg?

3. Why don't penguins get frostbite?

And *THEN*, when Mr. Bacon started taking attendance, I pretended I couldn't hear, so he had to say "Pippa Morgan" FOUR times, and then I answered in French and said *"bonjour"* instead of "here."

And *THEN*, while Mr. Bacon was handing out worksheets about our zoo trip, I started tap-dancing on the floor under my desk until Mr. Bacon told me to be quiet.

And *THEN*, I asked *more* questions, except this time I did it by singing:

1. ♫ "Why is it called a worksheet and not a work blanket?" ♫

2. ♫ "Why are there thirteen questions on the worksheet?" ♫

3 ♫ "Why is the number thirteen supposed to be unlucky?" ♫

I could tell Mr. Bacon was getting annoyed because he started ignoring my hand every time I raised it.

So I bounced up and down in my seat and waved my hand like I was desperate to go to the bathroom. And when he finally said, "What is it, Pippa?" I just shrugged and said, "I forgot."

It was all going well. Even Jason looked impressed. Then the terrible, horrible thing happened. Mr. Bacon suddenly slammed his whiteboard eraser on to his desk and said:

"PIPPA MORGAN, IF YOU DON'T STOP BEING SILLY, YOU CAN SPEND THE REST OF THE QUARTER NEXT TO JASON AT THE BOYS' TABLE!"

I heard Catie gasp, and she stared at me with pleading eyes and whispered, "Don't leave me!"
sobs heartbrokenly

WHAT AM I GOING TO DO?????

If I behave in class this afternoon	If I mess around in class this afternoon
I sit next to Catie for the rest of the quarter.	I sit with *boys* for the rest of the quarter.
I won't get into any more trouble.	Mr. Bacon will speak to Mom.
	Mom and Mr. B will fall in love and get married.
	Me, Mom, Mr. Bacon, and Saint Valentine will be happy.

This is the hardest decision I've ever made.

But Mom's happiness depends on me! I'm going to have to be brave, like the TV celebrities on *Help Me, I'm Famous!* They have to crawl through tunnels full of cockroaches to get food. If a celebrity can do that, then I can spend the rest of quarter sitting beside Jason Matlock so that Mom can get married by Valentine's Day.

Later—back at home

I did it.

I ignored Mr. Bacon during attendance and yelled across the class to Jason while Mr. Bacon was handing out worksheets. "Hey, Jason! I think I heard an ice-cream truck outside. Can you see?"

There was no way Jason could resist *that*. In a second, he was up and standing on his chair. "There's nothing there," he shouted, peering out of the window. "You're imagining things."

"I usually am!" I shouted back.

Mr. Bacon called it The Final Straw. (He

was practically purple with anger.) He shouted: "GET DOWN, JASON. AND PIPPA MORGAN—<u>TAKE YOUR BOOKS AND SIT AT THE BOYS' TABLE</u>!"

Everyone became very quiet. Jason got down off his chair. Catie squeezed my hand under the desk. I stared at Mr. Bacon and waited for him to go on. But he didn't. He just carried on handing out worksheets.

When I didn't move, he glared at me.

"NOW!"

Blushing as red as a flaming tomato, I gathered my books and moved my chair to the boys' table.

Jason was smirking at Tom as I squeezed in beside him.

AND THE WORST THING...

Mr. Bacon NEVER said he was going to speak to my mom!

I'd gotten myself into trouble for nothing, and I was going to spend the rest of the school year listening to Jason sniffing. I didn't dare look at Catie. If I saw her face, I knew I would cry.

Then, after the last bell, as I was putting

on my coat, Mr. Bacon walked into the coatroom.

"Come with me, Pippa Morgan! We'll wait on the playground together."

"Really?" I blinked at him in surprise. I felt my face turn pink as happiness exploded inside me.

I could hardly believe it!

He was going to speak to my mom.

It was SO HARD to stop myself from grinning as I followed him onto the playground. I nearly burst with excitement.

I could see the twins through the coatroom window doing a celebration dance. Catie was with them, staring out at me. I could tell she was wishing me luck.

"Is that your mom?" Mr. Bacon asked, scanning the sea of parents who were clustered like penguins around the school gates.

I followed his gaze, my heart booming with happiness.

Then I saw her.

OH NO!

My heart stopped booming and dropped into my boots.

Mom looked TERRIBLE! I'd completely forgotten that she was painting the kitchen today. Her hair was hidden under a ragged old scarf. Her face was splattered with yellow paint. She was wearing

Dad's old coveralls, which had rips in the elbows and knees.

I wondered whether to lie and tell Mr. Bacon I was supposed to walk home by myself today, but Mom was already zigzagging through the crowd toward me.

"Pippa! There you are!" She saw Mr. Bacon and stopped in front of us, frowning. "Is there something wrong?"

"I'd like a word, if you have time." Mr. Bacon pointed toward the front entrance.

Mom shot me a worried look and I smiled to reassure her, but she didn't look reassured as she followed Mr. Bacon into the classroom.

MR. BACON: (squeezing into one of the small

chairs beside Mandy Harrison's desk) Pippa's been acting up for the past couple of days.

MOM: *(squeezing into the chair opposite him)* Has she? *(They looked like clowns scrunched into a clown car.)*

ME: But I *had* to.

MR. BACON AND MOM TOGETHER: You *had* to?

ME: *(lying)* It was for my Valentine's project. One of the things I love is being silly. I was doing research on what it's like to be silly in school.

MR. BACON: But you disrupted the whole class.

ME: (pretending to look sorry) I didn't think about that.

MR. BACON: Then maybe you should have.

ME: Have you met my mom before, Mr. Bacon?

MOM: (answering first) We've met at parents' evening, Pippa.

ME: But you were with Dad then. He's never met you on your own before. (giving Mr. Bacon a meaningful look) He probably doesn't know that you're single now. And that you don't have a boyfriend right now.

MOM: (blushing through the specks of paint on her face) Pippa! Hush!

ME: But you're much more interesting than me. Look, Mr. Bacon. (pointing at her coveralls) Mom can do DIY. DIY means Do It Yourself.

MOM: (interrupting) Pippa!

ME: (ignoring her) She's painting the kitchen today. That's why she looks so bad. Normally she's much prettier. AND she's learning to cook. She invented fried pizza. It's delicious.

MR. BACON: (*smiling suddenly*) [It was almost like he'd guessed my plan. But he *couldn't* have. Old people never understand what's ***Facts*** going on.] I'm sure it is, Pippa. Your mom sounds like a wonderful woman, but we are here to talk about your behavior.

I started panicking because they were both looking at me, not each other. They hadn't fallen in love yet, so I scanned the classroom for things they might both like. But all I could see was the whiteboard. "We've got a whiteboard in our kitchen," I told Mr. Bacon desperately. "Mom uses it to make shopping lists. She has really neat whiteboard handwriting, just like yours."

127

Mom was staring at me like I'd gone crazy, but I went on anyway. "You two have so much in common. To begin with, you're both single. I don't think that grown-ups should be single. Did you know that it's nearly Valentine's Day?"

Mom's eyebrows shot up just like they did the time I tried to cut my own hair. "Pippa, are you trying to set me up with Mr.—"

Mr. Bacon interrupted. "Pippa is a lovely student, Mrs. Morgan. You must be very proud of her. I know she's been acting out for the last couple of days, but now that we've spoken, I can see that it's just been a blip."

A *blip*? I blinked at Mr. Bacon.

MR. BACON: I'm sure if you have a word with her (*raising his eyebrows and staring at Mom, like he's sending her secret messages with his eyes*) she'll be back to her usual self tomorrow.

MOM: (*raising her eyebrows and sending secret eye messages back, which is weird—it's like she's guessed my plan too*) I'm sure she will.

MR. BACON: Her math has really improved this quarter, and she's producing some excellent written work.

MOM: (*smiling*) She gets that from her dad. He's a wizard with numbers.

I stared at them, not believing my ears. Why were they talking about my schoolwork? Valentine's Day is THREE DAYS away! I'd brought them together and pointed out how much they have in common. Didn't they realize that they were meant to fall in love?

But Mom was already getting to her feet and shaking Mr. Bacon's hand. "Thank you for being so understanding."

Understanding? He hadn't understood at all! Neither of them had! But she went on.

"I'll have a talk with Pippa when we get home. I'm sure we can get this straightened out."

ME: Are we leaving already?

MOM: We need to get home; my paintbrushes are drying.

MR. BACON: One last thing.

My heart practically stopped. He was going to ask her out. I just knew it.

MR. BACON: I told Pippa that she'd have to sit at the boys' table for the rest of the school year, but now that we know why she's been acting up, I think she should sit beside Catie again.

But they *didn't* know why I'd been acting up! Not the *real* reason. If they did, they'd be planning their first date by now!

MOM: Thanks, Mr. Bacon.

Then she grabbed my hand and headed for the car. As I climbed into the passenger seat, I felt like I'd been pulled out of a movie halfway through. My thoughts were spinning. Maybe they *had* fallen in love and I'd missed it. Maybe that was what all the secret eye messages had been about. Maybe Mr. Bacon would phone Mom later and ask her out. Maybe Mom was already planning to send Mr. Bacon a Valentine's Day card.

I imagined him finding it on his desk and smiling as he opened it. Within weeks he'd announce the wedding, and everyone would crowd around me on the playground because *my* mom was marrying our teacher. And I could ask Catie to be a bridesmaid with me.

Then Mom interrupted my thoughts. "It was very sweet of you, Pippa."

I looked at her, puzzled. "What was?"

"Trying to get me and Mr. Bacon together."

I blushed. "You *knew?*"

Mom grinned. "He's a nice man, but I'm happy being single right now."

"Even though Dad has Faye?" Didn't she feel jealous?

"I'm glad your dad's happy," she told me. "And one day I might find someone I care about too, but right now I have plenty to make me happy." She ruffled my hair.

And that was it. Two days of school wasted on a plan that didn't work. *sigh* Mom is going to be alone forever. But she doesn't seem sad about it. She's painting the kitchen while I write in my diary. I can hear her rock music and she's singing along. Maybe I was wrong. Maybe she doesn't need a husband.

Grown-ups make NO sense. The good news is, we're having fish and chips for dinner because the oven's covered in plastic sheets.

Maybe it was lucky she and Mr. Bacon didn't fall in love. Imagine having a teacher for a stepdad. He'd probably give me extra homework and keep testing me on my math. And he'd expect me to get all the answers right in class. And I wouldn't be able to do my homework in front of the TV. And I couldn't make up excuses for why I hadn't finished it, because he'd know my goldfish wasn't sick or I hadn't really gotten locked out of the house and had to sleep in the car.

He'd probably put a whiteboard in every room and make me do spelling tests and

write out all the names of Henry VIII's wives. And I bet all of his friends are teachers. He'd ask them to come to dinner so that I'd be surrounded. The living room would be just like a teachers' lounge!

I bet he's best friends with Mr. Badger, our principal. Imagine—the school principal in *my* living room! Home would end up more like school—except I'd be the only pupil. My life would be the WORST!

AND I'D HAVE TO CHANGE MY NAME TO PIPPA *BACON*!!!!!!

Wow! I've had the luckiest escape ever. I'm so glad that it's just me and Mom. We have tons of fun together and she's the best mom in the world.

My stomach's rumbling. I'm going to see if it's time to go to the grocery store.

Wednesday, Feb. 12

I told Catie and the twins everything when I saw them at school. When Catie saw I was happy that Mr. Bacon wasn't going to be my stepdad, she laughed about Mom's paint-splattered outfit. The twins kept calling me Pippa Bacon, which was funny to start with, but then wasn't. Catie told them to stop teasing. (Catie always knows when I'm feeling embarrassed. That's why she's the best.) Then I told Catie I could sit next to her again, and we squealed and jumped up and down. I was extra good in class, and Mr. Bacon kept smiling at me. I wonder if he guessed that I had been trying to get him and Mom together?

On the way home from school, I asked Catie if we could stop at the park. I wanted to take some pictures of swings for my project. At the playground, I took a few pics of swings, but they were empty. It was drizzling and no one else was around, so the swings looked kind of sad. I asked Catie to sit on one so I could take some photos. I thought she was going to swing, but she just sat on it and dangled and dragged her toes along the ground.

ME: Don't you like swinging?

CATIE: It's boring.

ME: *(staring in amazement)* Boring?

CATIE: You just go up and down.

I gave Catie the camera and got on a swing. Swinging is NOT boring.

I showed her. I swung back and forth until I was going so high that my feet were pointing at the sky and my hair was trailing along the ground.

ME: I'm a rocket ship flying to the moon! I'm on a boat on gigantic waves! I'm a pendulum working the world's biggest clock.

Catie snapped some pictures. Then she sat on the swing beside me and started swinging. Before long she was going as high as me, and I changed my speed so that we were swinging together. Every time we rushed forward, my belly jumped into my throat, and when we swung back, my brain dropped down to my shoes.

Catie started whooping beside me. "This is fun!" I turned my head and saw her grinning. She stuck her legs out like sticks to fly even higher. "Swinging is definitely not boring when you swing like this!" she squealed. "I feel like I'm riding on a roller coaster!"

We were out of breath by the time we finished, and it was starting to get dark.

Catie asked if I wanted to go to her house, so we stopped at mine to ask Mom and she said yes, and we went to Catie's.

Mrs. Brown was in the kitchen when we got there. I could hear plates clattering, like she was emptying the dishwasher. I remembered to take off my shoes before walking across the perfectly polished hall floor. Catie poked her head around the kitchen door and told her mom I was here, and Mrs. Brown asked if I wanted to stay for dinner. All I could picture in my head was organic fish stew so I hesitated, but then Mrs. Brown added, "We're having chicken nuggets."

Catie grinned at me as I shouted, "Yes, please!" Then we ran upstairs to Catie's room and leapt across the white fluffy rugs that floated like clouds on her pink bedroom carpet.

Catie flopped on her bed and said, "What should we do?"

But I knew already. I wanted to hear Catie play her trombone. I could see the big black case she brought to school when there was band practice or a lesson. It was sticking out from under her bed. I hauled it out and looked at Catie with big puppy eyes. "Please play your trombone."

Catie blushed instantly, pinker than her bedspread. She'd never played in front of me before. "I get stage fright," she whispered.

"But you play at band practice and in lessons," I reasoned.

"That's different," Catie argued. "No one expects you to be great."

"I don't expect you to be great," I told her.

Catie looked at me, unconvinced.

So I sang for her.

I have the worst singing voice in the world. It's so bad, it's funny. Catie knows because she's seen me singing in a school show. Today, as soon as I started singing, Catie burst into giggles. She rolled over the bed, laughing, with her fingers in her ears.

So I stopped singing and said, "It can't be worse than that."

Catie sat up. "Nothing is worse than that!"

I flicked open her trombone case. "Go on, then," I dared. "Play."

Catie took the trombone out. She looked nervous. Standing on one of the fluffy white rugs, she put it to her lips.

She didn't look at me, and I sat quietly on the bed, trying to act like I wasn't really there so she wouldn't feel self-conscious.

Then she started blowing.

It was great! She didn't get all the notes right, but she really sounded fantastic.

When she'd finished, I told her, "You have to play it for your project!"

Catie stared at me. "No way! I'm just going to show a photo of it."

"What's the point of a trombone photo?" I argued. "Trombones are meant to be heard, not seen."

"I can't play in front of the whole class," Catie told me. "I'd die." She handed me the trombone. "Do you want to try?"

OF COURSE!

I took it off her and she tried to explain how to blow into it. You're supposed to do something funny with your lips or puff out your cheeks—I can't remember. I just remember blowing so hard my ears popped. And all that came out of the horn end was a sad hooting noise, like a whale crying.

Catie started laughing immediately.

So I tried again.

I imagined whales around the world hearing my sobs and heading for the coast to find out what was wrong.

Catie was laughing so hard, she couldn't speak. Tears were streaming from her eyes as she rolled around on the rug.

My lips *and* cheeks ached. "How do you

make it sound so nice?" I asked, putting the trombone back in its case.

Catie lay breathless on the carpet, still chuckling. "I practice," she hiccuped.

I sat on the bed and stared at her with a pretend-serious look. "I think I'm going to have to accept that I am just not musical."

Catie looked at me, and then collapsed into another fit of giggles. So I started thumping her with pillows and bashing her with fluffy pink cushions until I was giggling as loudly as she was.

When Mrs. Brown called us for chicken nuggets, I was the first downstairs. My nose was twitching like a puppy's, expecting to smell the familiar McDonald's smell. Instead, all I could smell was a homemade smell, like somebody had been cooking with *real* ingredients.

I sat down at the table nervously. What had Mrs. Brown done to my beloved chicken nuggets? Maybe she'd made them into an organic stew. As Catie sat next to me, looking excited, I whispered, "I thought we were having chicken nuggets."

Catie looked at her mom, who was carrying a big plate toward the table. She put it down, and I saw a pile of crispy lumps the size of golf balls. "Homemade chicken nuggets," Catie explained.

I stared in dread as Mrs. Brown told

me to help myself while she fetched the salads.

Catie put a nugget on my plate. "Try it."

Anxiously, I stabbed the mega-nugget with my fork. I took a bite, expecting it to taste like brown rice and blue cheese.

But guess what?

It tasted *fantastic*!

Almost as good as McDonald's!

I ate seven. And my salad.

I really think Mrs. Brown's cooking is improving. I'm going to ask Mom to give her the recipe for fried pizza. I think she may be ready for it.

Friday, Feb. 14

VALENTINE'S DAY!!!!

Today was the best day ever!

Mr. Bacon had decorated the classroom with pink streamers and balloons. The twins had both dressed in pink and Catie was wearing a pink ribbon in her hair. I wasn't wearing anything pink, because I don't have anything pink. But I am wearing my red jeans and a white T-shirt because if you mix red and white together you get pink. And I'd covered my Valentine's Day project folder with pink paper and drawn two pictures of Saint

Valentine on the front—one with his head on and one with his head missing, just to show how brave he was.

There was an envelope on everyone's desk, which we weren't allowed to open until after Mr. Bacon had taken attendance. They turned out to be Valentine's Day cards from famous people throughout history. Mine was from Henry VIII and it read, *I LOVE WIVES!* and Catie's was from Julius Caesar and it read, *Roses are red, violets are blue, I'm the best emperor Rome ever knew.*

We had to do math before recess because we *always* do math before recess on a Friday, but after recess we gave our Valentine's presentations.

My stomach was fluttering with butterflies. I'd practiced all last night. I hoped I wouldn't get my words mixed up.

Mr. Bacon let Darren start.

He talked about soccer players, Christmas, and hot dogs. Then Tom told us about his three favorite Xbox games. Then Julie and Jennifer performed some karate moves and did a karaoke song (which was really good), and then Mandy Harrison showed us 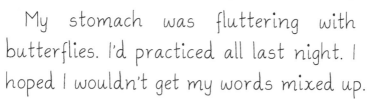 pictures of her dog and her gran and passed around her strawberry-scented lip balm. She said she didn't know which she loved best, but I hope it wasn't the lip balm, because when Jason got hold of it, he ate it.

Mandy Harrison tried to kick him, but Mr.

Bacon managed to slip in between them and made Jason promise to buy Mandy a new one.

Then it was my turn.

I stood up and opened my folder. First, I told everyone about swinging and how much fun it was to shoot up toward the stars like a rocket, and I showed them the pictures Catie had taken in the park. Then I told them about chicken nuggets and showed them the photo of Catie's nugget heart.

Then I told them about Mike Hatchett and how cool detectives were and how they should all definitely watch *CopShop*. And then I did the part I'd been rehearsing: I acted out my interview with the real detective we met at the zoo.

It was quite hard because I had to do different voices for him and me. And I'd brought props so every time I played the detective I had to quickly put on a hat and dark glasses. But I think it worked okay.

ME: (*using my real voice*) What's your name, rank, and badge number?

DET. BURROWS: (*putting on hat and glasses and using a deep policemanny voice*) Burrows, Detective, number 22244.

ME: (*taking off the hat and glasses and using my voice again*) Do you have a special detective badge?

DET. BURROWS: *(showing a badge I made out of some cardboard from an old cornflakes box)* Yes.

ME: What's the best thing about being a detective?

DET. BURROWS: Helping people.

ME: Would I make a good detective?

DET. BURROWS: Yes.

Then I bowed like a real actor—and my hat and glasses fell off. But everyone clapped. Especially Catie and the twins.

Mr. Bacon gave me a big smile as I sat down. "Thank you, Pippa. That was very informative and thoroughly researched." I grinned back at him proudly and said, "Thank you." Then he nodded at Catie. "Would you like to go next?"

Catie looked kind of nervous. Then I noticed a black case beside her chair. My stomach started butterflying excitedly. She'd brought her trombone! It wasn't her lesson today or band practice. Was she going to play?

Then I realized. She was probably just going to show the class what a real trombone looked like.

She talked about monkeys and showed everyone the picture I took of her being the

Monkey Queen. Then she talked about how much she loved playing the trombone. She undid her case and took it out. And just as I was expecting her to put it away again, she lifted it up to her lips and started playing.

It sounded <u>awesome</u>. And REALLY loud. I couldn't stop grinning.

But that wasn't the best part.

After she'd put her trombone away, she said, "I was going to tell you about my favorite color, but I changed my mind because there's something I love more than pink." She looked across the desk at Julie and Jennifer. "I love my friends. They make school feel like fun. I'm always happy when I'm with my friends."

Then she looked at me. "Especially when I'm with my *best* friend. Pippa Morgan."

I just stared back, happiness swelling in me like a big pink balloon.

Catie went on. "I love Pippa the best because she makes me do things I wouldn't normally do. She made me taste chicken nuggets for the first time and swing higher than I've ever dared before. It was Pippa who convinced me to play my trombone today. And last week she rescued me from a snake—even though it wasn't real, it *felt* real, but I knew that as long as Pippa was with me, I'd be okay."

I practically exploded with pride, and even though I was blushing, I didn't care.
I could hardly believe it!

Catie called me her BEST friend. It is totally official. Catie Brown and Pippa Morgan are BEST FRIENDS FOREVER!!! ☺ ☺ ☺

Later

Mom was waiting at the school gates for me. I gave her an extra-big hug because I was so happy and because it was Valentine's Day and she still wasn't married. We went to McDonald's and ate chicken nuggets as a special Valentine's Day treat.

Later, we watched a soppy movie called *Be My Valentine* about a man and woman who fall in love with each other while they're walking their dogs. I kept looking at Mom out of the corner of my eye to see if she was sad. It was her first Valentine's Day by herself. She *had* to be sad. But she didn't *look* sad. Every time one of the dogs in the movie did something cute, she laughed. And when the man and woman kissed for the first time, she looked all gooey. Then she put her arm around me and gave me a squeeze and said, "How about a Valentine's Day chocolate?" and I said, "Do we have chocolate?" and she pulled out a big pink box of truffles from under the sofa and said, "Of course! You can't have Valentine's Day without chocolate!"

And I asked, "Even if you don't have a valentine?"

And she said, "Chocolate is the best valentine there is."

Which is totally true.

Best. Valentine. Ever.

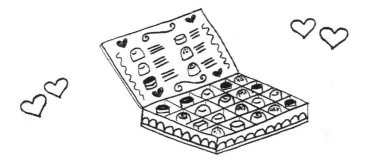

MOM'S RECIPE FOR FRIED PIZZA*

1. Take one store-bought pizza and remove the packaging.

2. Accidentally drop pizza on the floor.

3. Quickly pick it up and shout "three second rule!" (According to Mom, if you drop something on the floor and pick it up within three seconds, germs don't have enough time to get on to it. I didn't realize germs moved so slowly. But I guess if you're a germ and a humungous pizza drops on your head you're going to be too shocked to move for a while.)

4. Totally ignore the instructions on the packaging about putting the pizza in the oven.

5. Heat up a frying pan and put the pizza in there instead.

6. When smoke starts coming from the pizza, remove it from the pan.

7. Scrape the burnt parts off the bottom of the pizza and eat.

* Mom says only grown-ups should fry pizza, so please don't try this at home!

PIPPA MORGAN'S: HOW TO BE A DETECTIVE

You have to be really good at noticing things—especially suspicious things.

This can be hard because most bad guys try not to look suspicious. They don't go marching down the road shouting, "I'm going to rob a house," or, "Hooray! I just robbed a bank!"

So you have to look out for telltale clues, like looking sort of nervous or having shifty eyes. (I'm not exactly sure what "shifty eyes" means, but one time when my mom's best friend Sally saw a man stealing some sausages from the supermarket, she said, "I could tell he was up to no good because he had really shifty eyes.")

You have to be good at asking questions.

Detectives have to interview suspects all the time.

Detective Mike Hatchett from *CopShop* is great at interviewing suspects. His favorite question is: "Are you lying to me, sonny?"

This is a really cool question. One time, when I thought Mom was fibbing about there being no chocolate cookies left, I said, "Are you lying to me, sonny?" and she started to laugh and then she went and got me a chocolate cookie!

You must want to help other people.

Detectives help all kinds of people. They don't just keep us safe from criminals, they do lots of other cool stuff too, like helping old ladies cross the road and giving people directions when they get lost. They also go to schools and give talks.

When P. C. Buckley came to our school to give a talk about stranger danger, I asked him thirteen-and-a-half questions. (Mr Bacon stopped me halfway through my fourteenth question because he said I had to let other people have a chance.)

PIPPA MORGAN'S
ODE TO CHICKEN NUGGETS

Oh, chicken nuggets,

you're so yummy.

I love it when you fill my tummy.

Your crunchy coating,

your tasty meat.

You are my favorite mealtime treat.

Dunked in ketchup,

eaten with fries.

In any contest you win first prize.

Oh, chicken nuggets,

you're so delish.

Eating you is my biggest wish!